TYING FLIES

WORKSTATION

WORKSTATION *is a new concept
comprising all the elements
you need to begin tying flies.*

*The first 48 pages explain
the basic techniques of tying flies, and
includes details of a number of sample
flies that can be tied using the tools
and equipment supplied in this
book. Additional pages of
recipes for flies are provided
at the back of the book.*

BRIAN GROSSENBACHER

PRICE STERN SLOAN

Los Angeles

A PRICE STERN SLOAN—
DESIGN EYE BOOK

© 1996 Design Eye Holdings Ltd.
Produced by Design Eye Holdings Ltd.
First published in the United States
by Price Stern Sloan; Inc., A member of
The Putnam & Grosset Group,
New York, New York.

ISBN 0-8431-7974-0

First Edition
1 3 5 7 9 10 8 6 4 2

Printed in China

Illustrations by Adam Abel

Warning:
This product is intended as a beginner's
guide for ages 8 and up. Children under
8 years of age should be strictly supervied
by an adult.

CONTENTS

INTRODUCTION

TYING FLIES is both an art and a craft: Precise skills of fabrication are used to serve as a practical end. Fine materials are tied, woven, spun, and clipped into delicate creations for the purpose of fooling wary fish to take a hook. The ultimate judge of a well-tied fly is not the owner of a fly shop, the editor of a fly-fishing magazine, nor a guide on a famous river. No, the adjudicator is out there right now, finning anxiously in the swift current of an icy mountain stream or cruising the shallows of a mossy lake alertly searching for its next feeding opportunity. The act of fooling a cunning brown trout, a crafty bass, or an aggressive pike on a hand-tied fly is the true measure of success in this discipline.

Tying flies is easy. Perhaps its most appealing element is the fact that even the novice tier can achieve immediate results. Several effective flies are quite easy to reproduce and can be tied with minimal experience. As you build your skills, each new technique can be combined with another to create completely different flies. There are no boundaries in fly-tying. Experimentation, not only with regard to technique, but in terms of materials and style, also continually build and improve the sport.

This is the ultimate arbiter of whether a fly has been well-tied or not.

A photograph that captures the magic and allure of fly-fishing.

Tying flies is relaxing. Imagine fishing your favorite waters without even leaving your desk. Flies themselves summon up their own indelible memories of past fishing trips. Each winter the images of the upcoming season can be associated with the tying of particular flies . . . the subtle twitch of a Dave's hopper followed by an inhaling swirl of a wild Yellowstone trout taking the fly . . . streamer fishing (i.e. fishing with a fly that imitates a living baitfish) for aggressive brown trout as the last colors of autumn fade from the cottonwood trees . . . the resonant plunk of a deer-hair frog fly splashing on a marshy farm pond, punctuated by the charging v-wake of a hungry largemouth bass. Fly-tying conjures up fond memories of fishing and excites dreams of anticipation of future journeys to the water.

People tie flies for a variety of reasons. Some do it as a practical means of stocking their fly boxes. Others tie flies because they enjoy the challenge of fooling a fish with a lure of their own creation. Some fly-tiers do not even fish, but choose to tie flies simply as a relaxing pastime or as an outlet for their artistic nature. Regardless of your reason, tying flies can offer years of satisfaction and enjoyment. Even for an experienced practitioner, it remains a challenge—there is always room for improvement.

This is a scene that has been enacted over many centuries of the sport.

Your first catch with a homemade fly is a moment to savor.

The History of Fly-tying

Although fly-fishing and fly-tying have enjoyed a great boom in popularity over the last twenty years, elements of the sport can be traced back historically for well over a thousand years. The earliest known use of hand-tied flies dates back to the 2nd century C.E. when, in De Natura Animalium, the Roman writer Claudius Aelianus described swarms of caddis flies over the Astraeus river and alluded to the use of artificial flies by the Macedonians to catch trout and grayling. Much later, in the 17th century, the best known written account of early fly-tying is provided by Charles Cotton who contributed a chapter to the 1676 edition of Izaak Walton's *The Compleat Angler*. In this, Cotton examines the relationship between aquatic insect biology and fly-fishing. Today, the abundance of tools and materials on the market afford fly-tiers much greater versatility and scope for invention, and it is no surprise to see the explosive increase in creative and realistic fly patterns that are currently available. "Flies," as Dave Whitlock candidly describes them, "complete with eyeballs, elbows and arseholes." Many of these newer patterns and materials have changed the sport considerably. As you begin to tie flies, welcome these new patterns and materials with open arms, but do not underestimate the productivity of classic flies on which the sport has been built. These timeless wonders, such as the Pheasant Tail Nymph, the Adams Dry Fly, and the Woolly Bugger, will still be catching fish when our grandchildren look back and wonder how on earth we were ever able to cast our outdated graphite

A finished fly must look real enough to lure a fish.

WHAT IS A FLY?

THE TERM "tying flies" is something of a misnomer. Sure, many of the patterns do imitate the appearance of flies, but other "flies" are tied that resemble baitfish, terrestrials (land-born insects that are commonly blown into the water), snails, and even frogs. Under the broad definition of "tying flies," we will break down the categories into three major sections; **Nymphs, Dry Flies,** and **Streamers**.

There are thousands of species of aquatic insects. Fly-tiers aim to mimic their appearance using artificial materials.

Nymphs

A nymph or wet fly imitates the larval and pupal form of aquatic insects. The word "nymph" is a scientific term for one of the stages in an insect's development. Nymphs live below the surface of the water, therefore the hand-tied imitations are typically streamlined and weighted so they will sink quickly. A dry fly floats on the surface of the water and is tied to imitate the winged, adult stage of aquatic insects and terrestrials.

Nymph Red Bellied Girdle Fly

Dry flies

Dry flies are tied on fine wire hooks and use tightly-wound hackle, hollow-shafted hair follicles, or foam to support their weight on the surface of the water. (The term "hackle" refers to an individual feather that, when wrapped around the hook, flares its fibers in 360° spirals rather like the bristles of a bottle brush.) Examples of these are adult mayflies, caddis flies, beetles, and grasshoppers.

Dry fly Parachute Adams

Streamers

A streamer is any baitfish, frog, or crayfish imitation that is fished actively with some type of retrieval motion that causes the fly to move in a life-like manner. Examples of streamers include minnows, sculpin, and leeches.

Streamer Woolly Bugger

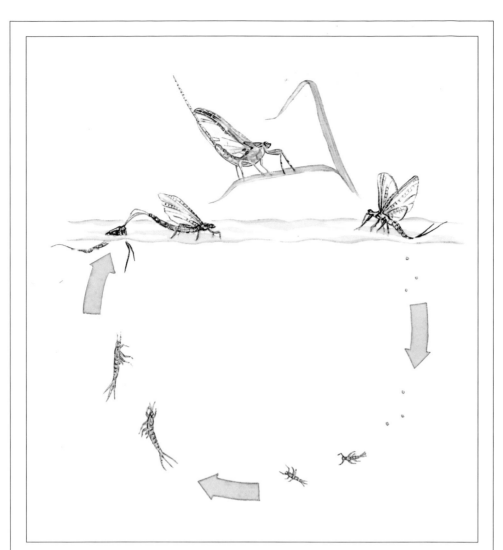

The world of aquatic insects is as fascinating as the fish that feed on them. Virtually every rock in a stream, lake, or pond is a home to some type of aquatic life. There are thousands of species of aquatic insects and this variation in species is matched by corresponding differences in size, shape, color, and behavior. Couple this with the countless species of baitfish, terrestrials, frogs, and other aquatic life upon which fish feed and you may become overwhelmed just by trying to decide what fly to use.

Matching the hatch

The key is what fisherman and fly-tiers refer to as "matching the hatch." Fish are opportunists and will eat not only what is the most prevalent source of food, but also what is the easiest for them to forage. As a fly-tier you will quickly become a stream-side observer. Go to your local

Mayfly life cycle
Mayfly eggs hatch into nymphs. This stage lasts from a few months up to two years, then the nymphs ascend to the surface and hatch or emerge as duns. Duns then fly up into the streamside vegetation, where they shed their skin to become spinners. And so the cycle repeats.

fishing water and look under the rocks. Pick up sticks on the river bottom. Use a fine-mesh net or a small piece of window screen to collect insects and other aquatic life. Take some collection jars with you to catalog your samples to use for later reference. Pay particular attention to the size, shape, and color of aquatic insects and other life forms. Once you discover a plentiful food source in the locality, then you are ready to imitate that source by tying flies. The ability to recreate your stream-side observations with hand-tied flies greatly tips the scales in your favor as an angler.

TOOLS OF THE TRADE

THE FIRST REQUIREMENTS for tying a good fly are quality tools and materials. This chapter will introduce you to the basic tools and materials used in tying flies.

Vise

The vise is the most important tool which is included in your Workstation. Its purpose is to hold hooks securely while giving you ample room to manipulate tools and materials around the hook shank. When placing the hook in the vise, use care to anchor only the bend of the hook between the jaws. If too much of the hook is placed into the vise, then you risk

Anchor only the bend of the hook in the jaws of the vise or it may be damaged.

damaging the hook. If too little of the hook is placed in the vise, then it will not be held securely.

Bobbin

The bobbin can be viewed as an extension of your fingers. It holds spooled thread firmly and allows you to wind the thread on the fly both securely and accurately. To thread the bobbin, place the spool between the posts, so that the brass tips fit securely into the round holes of the thread spool. Unwind 4–6 in. (10–15 cm.) of thread from the spool and carefully push it through the neck of the bobbin. If the thread does not go all the way through

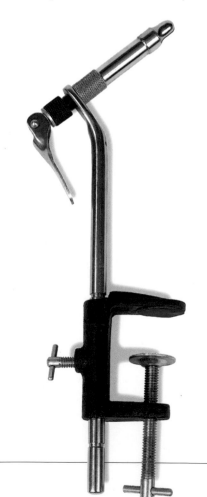

Thread just entering the neck—notice the direction of the thread and its moistened tip.

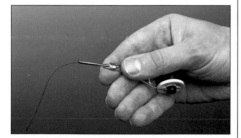

The bobbin is held in the palm of your hand with the neck supported by thumb and forefinger.

when you feed it by hand, place your lips on the opposite side of the bobbin neck and suck the thread through. The bobbin is held in the palm of your hand, with the neck of the bobbin supported by your thumb and forefinger (see photograph above). In this way, tension may be applied to the spool simply by closing your hand around the spool.

Scissors

A sharp pair of scissors with fine points is crucial to achieving the crisp, precise cuts necessary in fly-tying. Try to get into the habit of holding your scissors in your bobbin hand while you are tying. This way they are always available and do not get lost in the assortment of materials and tools spread out on your desk. Quality scissors should not be used to cut heavy wire or tinsel. Use a cheaper pair of scissors for cutting coarse materials.

Bodkin

The bodkin is a needle-type tool that is used to apply head cement to the fly and to pick out the dubbing used to create the effect of life-like gills and legs on various patterns. The needle point may also be used to clean the eye of the hook if any errant head cement should block it.

Half-hitch tool

The bodkin supplied in the Workstation also has a half-hitch tool built into the handle. The half-hitch tool simply helps you place a series of cinching (or binding) loops onto the hook shank so that the finished fly will not come untied. If used correctly, the half-hitch tool is both quicker and easier than most whip-finishing tools. This tool is conveniently shaped as a hexagon so that it will not roll off your table.

Although the following items are not included in the Workstation, they give you an inventory of specialized tools that may be used to complete some of the more advanced techniques covered later in this book. You may want to invest in them as your technique improves and your confidence grows.

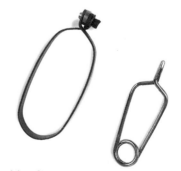

Hackle pliers

Hackle pliers are used to grip small pieces of materials and to hold them securely while you wrap them around the fly. There are several types of hackle pliers on the market but look for ones that have one rubber and one metal tip. These have the greatest gripping power.

Hair stacker

To align the individual fibers of hair wings on a fly, a hair stacker must be used. A hair stacker consists of a tube that fits snugly inside a cylinder with a flat

bottom. The individual shafts of hair are placed inside the tube, tips down. Both the tube and the cylinder should be rapped on the table a few times to even the hairs. Now turn the tube and cylinder sideways and slowly remove the tube from the cylinder. The hairs should be evenly stacked and ready for tying. ***Note:*** *Stiff guard hairs and irregularly long hairs may be easily separated and discarded at this stage.*

Dubbing pick

A dubbing pick is used to "tease" out the stiffer guard hairs of a fly to give a life-like impression of legs or gills. A practical dubbing pick can be made by wrapping a piece of adhesive Velcro around the end of a toothpick, or gluing a strip of Velcro to a thin piece of emery board. Use the dubbing pick as a type of hairbrush to tease out the dubbing until you achieve the desired effect.

Dubbing twister

A dubbing twister can be used to twist the dubbing between two strands of thread. This can be especially useful if you want to accentuate the stiffer guard hairs and create an extremely fuzzy fly. A dubbing twister can be created at home simply by bending a paperclip into a hook shape.

A homemade dubbing pick made of a piece of Velcro wound around a piece of emery board.

Head cement

Head cement or lacquer may be used to give the head of the fly a shiny coating and added strength. Although a properly finished head does not need lacquer, it

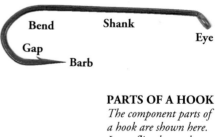

does add to the aesthetic appeal of the fly. ***Note:*** *Clear fingernail polish is a readily available substitute for head cement.*

Hooks

The hook is the building block of the fly. It can be divided into five major sections: the eye, shank, bend, barb, and gap. The components of the hook may be used as measurement gauges to help ensure the proper proportions of your flies. As a general rule, the tail of dry flies and streamers should be about the same length as the hook shank. The wing for a dry fly will also be the length of the hook shank. The tail of a nymph will be the length of the hook gap.

Bend Shank Eye
Gap Barb

PARTS OF A HOOK
The component parts of a hook are shown here. Large flies demand heavier-shanked hooks than are used for many of the dry flies.

Shapes and varieties

Hooks come in all shapes and sizes. Fine wire hooks are used for dry flies, while heavier shanked hooks are used for nymphs and streamers for added strength and weight. Curved-shanked hooks can be used to imitate swimming or wiggling nymphs. Long-shanked hooks are typically used in tying streamers. As a novice fly-tier you may find the huge selection of hooks on the market rather overwhelming. At this point, keep your hook selection simple. Don't become

Dry Fly Hooks *#10–20 Note lighter construction for greater buoyancy.*

Streamer Hooks *#2–10 Note long shank and heavy construction.*

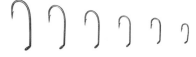

Nymph Hooks *#8–18 Note the heavier construction.*

Bass Hooks *#2/0–1 #2 Note short shank and wide hook gap for greater hooking power.*

Scud/Curved Nymph Hooks *#8–18 Curved hook helps imitate wriggling nymphs.*

overly concerned with specialty hooks. For now focus only on the size and weight of hooks. If you are tying dry flies, then use a light wire hook (typically denoted a 1x fine). If you are tying nymphs and streamers use a heavier gauge hook (1x heavy).

The size of hooks is measured on an even numbered scale. As the number gets larger, the hook size gets smaller— for example a #2 hook is much larger than a # 10 hook. Standard hook sizes range from a # 2 to # 20.

CATCH AND RELEASE TIP

Using barbless hooks or simply crimping shut the barb on your hooks dramatically reduces the risk of injury to the fish, decreases the need to handle fish as the hook is much more easily extracted, and will make you thankful when your line is accidentally hooked in the back of your expensive new fishing vest.

Crimping tool.

Barbless hooks reduce the need to handle fish.

Each of these spools hold thread of a different diameter. Shown in the center is kevlar thread.

Thread

Like the hook, thread is an important component of every hand-tied fly. It is used to anchor materials to the hook shank and to hold the fly together. When selecting thread for a particular fly, the tier should carefully consider its strength and diameter. As a general rule, use the finest thread that can be handled on the fly without breaking. Thread diameter is denoted by the number of zeros listed on the label—the greater the number of zeros, the finer the thread. For example, heavy gauge thread for nymphs and streamers is denoted as 3/0 or three zeros. This is a large diameter thread that is best used for bigger flies that can carry the extra bulk and that require strength to anchor coarse materials. Medium-sized dry flies and nymphs are best tied with 6/0 thread which offers a nice balance between strength and moderate diameter. Smaller dry flies should be tied with fine 8/0 thread which allows for a crisp, trim design without a build-up of unnecessary bulk. Kevlar thread can be used for flies that require ultra-high breaking strength, such as spun hair flies, and large bass and pike flies. Kevlar thread is virtually unbreakable; it is made from the same material that is used in lightweight bullet-proof vests. Do note, however, that kevlar thread may groove your bobbin and blunt your scissors.

Left: *Fishing at dusk and they are biting!*

Right: *Large-sized dry flies, nymphs, and streamers are best tied with 3/0 thread.*

FLY-TYING MATERIALS

F LY-TYING materials are as diverse as the
people who tie flies. Would you
believe that a popular Western stonefly
pattern was originally tied with legs made
from rubber that came from the elastic
waistband of an unsuspecting wife's
girdle? The name of the fly—The Girdle
Bug. Fly-tying materials can be
divided into the two major
categories of natural and
synthetic. Natural materials
include feathers, fur, and hair.
Synthetics include yarns, floss, tinsel,
wire, beads, foam, and rubber. This
section of the book lists some common
fly-tying materials and gives a brief
description of their principal uses.

Natural materials

Virtually any type of feather may be used
in fly-tying. From peacock to ostrich,
surprising effects can be achieved by using
these unique feathers. Many feathers are
put to highly specialized use and the
business of genetic breeding to create
birds with feathers of a particular type has
become quite successful. The best
example of this is hackle feathers. The
term *hackle* in fly-tying has a dual
meaning. It refers both to the saddle and
neck feathers of genetically bred chickens
and to the spiraled feathers wound tightly
around the thorax section of dry flies that
help keep them afloat.

Quality hackle feathers come from the

*Quality hackle
feathers come from the
neck and saddle
regions of specially
bred chickens.*

Parts of a tied fly.

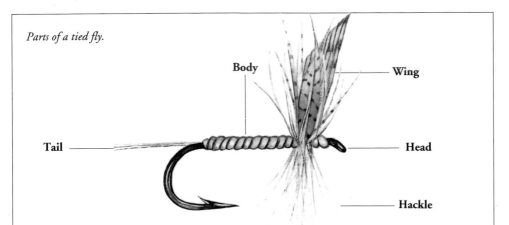

Body

Wing

Tail

Head

Hackle

neck and back portions of specially bred and selected chickens. Hackle feathers are wrapped around the hook shank causing the individual feather barbules to stick straight out like the bristles on a bottle brush. The hackle is used to keep dry flies afloat and to impart an undulating movement to a submerged nymph or streamer. High quality neck hackle offers stiff fibers that are of consistent length along the entire feather shaft. The short, stiff fibers from a neck hackle can be spun around the body and thorax (the section of the insect between the head and the abdomen) of a dry fly to help support its weight on the surface of the water, as well as to imitate the bristly legs of an insect. Although expensive, a quality neck hackle is worth every cent. It should last you several seasons of tying—it should have

hundreds of usable feathers on it, and it will give your flies a clean, crisp look as well as exceptional buoyancy.

The saddle hackle refers to the portion of feathers that drape over the back of the bird. Compared to neck hackle, the saddle typically has long, soft feathers. Saddle hackle is often used for nymphs and streamers, because the longer hackle fibers impart life-like movements to the fly underwater, and because they are usually too soft to support the weight of a fly on the surface of the water and so are inappropriate for dry flies. However, some companies have recently developed lines of saddle hackle that have the qualities conducive to tying impressive dry flies. These can be cost-efficient alternatives to the expensive neck hackles described above.

Wrapping a dry-fly hackle.

Saddle hackle on nymph (Bead Head Prince).

Hackles on dry fly (Royal Wulff).

Saddle hackle on streamer (Bead Head Spruce).

OTHER FEATHERS

1 Pheasant tail
This chocolate-brown feather is best known for its namesake fly—the Pheasant Tail Nymph. However, this versatile material can also be used for dry-fly wings, nymph thoraxes, and as tail fibers for a variety of flies. ***Note:*** *Pheasant tail will become brittle with age, so only buy what you can use in one season.*
Suggested Uses:
• Body and thorax of Pheasant Tail Nymph
• Wing for Henryville Caddis

2 Turkey flat
This broad, heavy feather from the rump of the bird can be used to create rugged wingcases for large stonefly nymphs.

Similar to the pheasant tail, the turkey flat can be used for dry-fly wings and nymphal thoraxes. For extra durability, turkey flat may be coated with head cement before use.
Suggested Uses:
• Wing case for Kaufmann's Stone, Hare's Ear Nymph

3 Ostrich herl
These soft feathers, which are also commonly used as household dusters, can be wrapped around the hook shank to create soft, billowing bodies or heads of caddis emergers. An *emerger* is a transitional form of an insect as it changes from nymph to adult.
Suggested Uses:
• Head for Peeking Caddis
• Body for Damselfly Nymph

2

1

3

4 Peacock herl/sword

If there was ever an award for the most valuable fly-tying material, peacock would win hands down. The term *herl* refers to the barbs of the eye feathers of a male peacock. The metallic green sheen of this versatile feather gives it a unique buggy hue. Used commonly in dry flies, nymphs, and streamers, peacock is both affordable and easy to use.

Suggested Uses:
• Body for Prince Nymph, Royal Wulff, Zug Bug
• Thorax for Pheasant Tail Nymph
• Underbody for Peacock Beetle

5 Marabou

This soft, plumy feather, originally derived from marabou storks and now taken from turkeys, simply takes on a living characteristic underwater. It pulsates, throbs, undulates, and just drives fish crazy.

Suggested Uses:
• Tail for Woolly Bugger
• Wing for Marabou Muddler
• Body for Damselfly Nymph

6 Goose biots

These short barbules on the front edge of goose wing feathers are commonly used for tying wings, legs, and tails of nymphs. Additionally they may be wrapped around the hook shank to create a segmented "quill" effect that mimics the look of the body of dry flies.

Suggested Uses:
• Tail and wing for Prince Nymph
• Legs for Golden Stone
• Tails for Kaufmann Stone

4

5

6

HAIR AND FUR

1 Deer and elk hair

Deer and elk hair are appreciated by fly-tiers because of their remarkable buoyancy which is the result of the individual hair follicles having hollow shafts. The air inside helps them float. They can be used interchangeably for dry-fly wings and may be spun and clipped to create a variety of shapes for bodies and heads of larger flies.

Suggested Uses:
• Wings for Elk Hair Caddis, Comparaduns
• Tail for Royal Wulff
• Spun hair flies such as the Dahlberg Diver

2 Calf tail/body

The stunning white hair from the tail and body of a calf possesses a unique translucent quality that makes it a favorite tail-and-wing material for some of the most popular western dry flies. Calf body/tail is popular among fisherman who demand an ultra-high-visibility fly.

Suggested Uses:
• Wings for Royal Wulff, Royal Trude, Parachute Adams
• Tail for H&L Variant

3 Muskrat

This soft, water-repellent fur can be clipped from the hide of a muskrat to create a naturally buoyant dubbing with stiff guard hairs that create very life-like impressions of an insect's legs.

Suggested Uses:
• Body dubbing for Adams/Parachute Adams

4 Rabbit fur/hare's mask

Best known for the effects given by the stiff guard hairs, rabbit fur is a natural material for nymphs that require a definite body shape embellished by the many legs and gills of an aquatic insect. The softer underfur dubs nicely, allowing the tier to taper the body and thorax, while the longer guard hairs mimic the appearance of gills and legs.

Suggested Uses:
• Dubbing for Hare's Ear Nymph
• Body for Peeking Caddis, Scud imitations

5 Moose hair

These long, dark hairs can be used as tail fibers for both nymphs and dry flies as well as for fabricating remarkably life-like legs for beetles and crickets. This ultra-stiff fiber maintains its body even when wet.

Suggested Uses:
• Tail for Royal Wulff
• Legs for Peacock Beetle

6 Red squirrel fur

This soft fur can be clipped and used as a soft dubbing for a variety of dry-fly and nymphal imitations.

Suggested Uses:
• Body for Red Fox Nymph, Hendrickson
• Body for Ginger Fox dry fly

SYNTHETICS

1 Floss, tinsel, wire

These materials are used to rib fly bodies for color contrast, strength, and sheen. Ribbing refers to the act of wrapping material around the body of a fly.

Suggested Uses:

(Floss)
- Body band for Royal Wulff
- Body for Yellow/Red Humpy

(Tinsel)
- Ribbing for Prince Nymph, Hare's Ear, Zug Bug
- Body for Mickey Finn

(Wire)
- Ribbing for Woolly Bugger
- Counter rib for Pheasant Tail Nymph
- Body for Brassie

2 Chenille

This furry, string-like yarn can be used to create a variety of body shapes and colors for streamers and large nymphs. Chenille is quite durable and easy to use which makes it an old favorite among fly-tiers.

Suggested Uses:
- Body for Woolly Worm/Woolly Bugger
- Body for Bitch Creek Nymph

3 Dubbing

There are countless colors, textures, and uses for synthetic dubbing. Dubbing is applied to the thread with a tacky wax and both are then wrapped around the hook shank to create realistic bodies, heads, and thoraxes. Synthetic dubbing can be used for both dry and wet flies.

Suggested Uses:
- Body material for Elk Hair Caddis, Comparadun
- Underbody for Sparkle Pupa
- Body for Janssen's Crayfish

4 Crystal flash/Flashabou

These ultra-thin strips of mylar add pizazz to any fly pattern. They can be wrapped

1

2

3

as "ribbing" for a fly, blended with the extended tail of a streamer to add a life-like flash of color, or they can be folded over the thorax of nymphs to create a "flashback" effect.

Suggested Uses:
• Blended with marabou to form the tail of Woolly Bugger
• Wing casing for Flashback Hare's Ear and Pheasant Tail Nymph

5 Antron/Z-lon

These super-tough poly-fibers were originally created as carpet yarns; however, they can be used to make realistic segmented bodies, loose fiber tails, and life-like sparkle wings. Both antron and Z-lon have a shiny, translucent quality that make them ideal for mimicking aquatic insect life.

Suggested Uses:
• Body for Serendipity
• Tail for Sparkle Dun
• Outer body for Sparkle Pupa

6 Foam (not illustrated)

This can be used to imitate virtually any part of a fly. The wide variety of colors in which it is available and its natural buoyancy make it an extremely valuable material to fly-tiers. Look for closed-cell foam for dry flies and open-cell foam for nymphs and streamers. Closed-cell foam has closed chambers that trap air and cause it to float, while open-cell foam absorbs water and sinks easily.

Suggested Uses:
• Body for Foam Hopper
• Body for High Vis Beetle
• Body for Foam Ant

Note:

Do not think that you can only use materials that are commercially available. Some of the most effective patterns are tied with common materials that can be found at craft stores or even around the house. From carpet yarn to girdles, new materials are being discovered everyday.

4

5

STORING AND MAINTAINING YOUR EQUIPMENT

Set up your fly-tying desk in an area that is both comfortable and well-lit. The two most important pieces of equipment in fly-tying are a comfortable chair and a good light. If you have these two items, you can sit and tie comfortably for hours without suffering from unnecessary eye fatigue or back pain.

A flat desk with plenty of available work area will make it easier to lay out your tools and keep better track of your materials. A piece of 2 ft. x 2 ft. (60 cm. x 60 cm.) green felt may be used to protect the table top from accidental spills of head cement. The green color provides an excellent background that is easy on the eyes, while the soft felt will protect your tools if you happen to drop any of them. Lay out your materials in order of their

use for a particular fly. This not only aids in organization, but serves as a reminder of the order of materials you will need for a given fly. To keep your desk clean, a small bag can be taped to its edge, just below the vise, to catch scraps of fur, thread, and other discarded materials. A magnet can be used to hold a supply of hooks so they will not be inadvertently swept into your trash receptacle or lost among other materials.

Storage

As the quantity of materials and equipment that you possess increases, so does the need for a safe and organized method of storage. Patches of fur and feathers are favorite playthings for cats and dogs. These are best kept in resealable bags, rectangular plastic food containers, or stored in multi-drawer nut/bolt boxes that can be purchased inexpensively at a hardware store. Hooks can be kept in plastic craft boxes with dividers to separate them by size, style, and weight. Tools can be kept in a zippered wallet or a wooden block with a variety of holes of different gauges drilled to accommodate the various items. Some people build desk-top trays that are designed to store all of their tools and materials so that when they are done tying, they can simply move the tray off the desk and out of the way. Your methods of organization and storage will greatly depend on your personal preference. Simply aim to develop a system that works for you.

Top *Tools can be kept in a wooden block.*
Above *Hooks arranged neatly in a fly box.*

FLY-TYING TECHNIQUES

This chapter is designed to give you an understanding of some of the many techniques that are used when tying flies. These techniques are initially quite simple, but then get progressively more difficult. Each of these techniques builds on the previous ones.

Anchoring thread to the hook

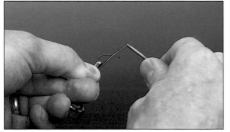

1) To anchor thread to the hook, pinch the loose end of thread between the thumb and forefinger of your left hand while holding the bobbin in your right. Maintain tension on the thread with both hands.

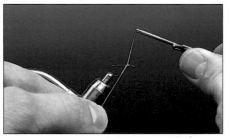

2) Position your left hand below the hook shank, and the bobbin above the hook shank.

3) Wrap the bobbin end of the thread ·

around the hook shank in a clockwise motion. Continue this motion until you have placed a minimum of five wraps around the hook shank—each wrap covering the tag end of the thread. Cut or break off the remaining tag end.

The half-hitch

The half-hitch tool may be used as an efficient alternative to whip-finish the heads of flies. This tool helps to thread a loop placed over the eye of the hook. Half hitches should be applied in pairs so they will cinch up tightly against one another to make a secure binding.

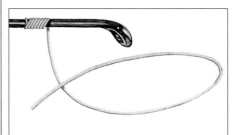

1) Forming the loop.

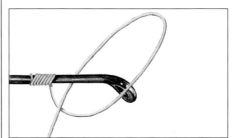

2) Placing loop over shank.

3) Cinching down finished hitch.

Weighting a fly

Wet flies, nymphs, and streamers typically require some type of secondary weight to help them sink to the depth that you would like to fish. A method that has gained popularity in recent years is to simply slip a brass bead over the bend of the hook and slide it to the eye of the hook, where it will stop and remain exposed as the head of the fly.

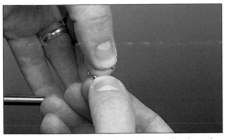

1) Simply slip a brass bead over the bend.

Note: Pinching shut the barb of the hook will make it considerably easier to slip the bead over the bend of the hook. These bead-head flies sink rapidly, and offer additional flash to the fly by simulating the gaseous bubbles that often form under the nymphal shuck of emerging insects.

Barbell eyes

Barbell eyes can confer life-like appearance to any streamer pattern as well as adding significant weight to the front of the fly which creates an irresistible undulating motion when the fly is stripped actively through the current. Barbell eyes can be securely anchored to the hook using figure-eight wraps for eight to ten repetitions, and then tightened by circling the wraps with thread above the hook shank, but below the eyes. Repeat this entire process twice more and then whip-finish. Coating the wraps with epoxy or head cement will add significantly to their durability.

1) Anchoring eyes to the hook shank.

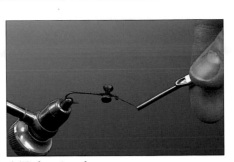

2) Tightening the wraps.

Using lead wire

Using lead wire to weight a fly gives the tier a tremendous amount of versatility and control. To adjust the weight of any particular fly, you can vary the diameter of the lead wire, as well as the amount and placement of the lead. For a small nymph (size 12–16), you would want to use a small diameter lead wire (0.015 in.); for medium flies (size 8-12), a medium diameter (0.02–0.025 in.); and for large flies (size 2–6), you would want to use a heavy diameter (0.03–0.035 in.). For best results wrap the lead over a base of thread on the hook shank. This will help the wire grip the shank firmly so the finished fly will not rotate around the hook. Lead wire can be wrapped along for the entire length of the hook shank, or merely near the head of the fly to help build up the thorax.

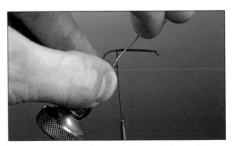

1) Wrap the lead over a base of thread on the hook shank.

2) Lead wire can be wrapped along the entire hook shank for a heavy fly.

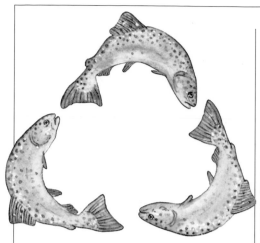

use the index finger of your left hand to even the tips of the fibers by tapping them. Once even, measure them to the shank of the hook. As a standard rule, the tail of a fly should be the same length as the shank of the hook.

3) With the thumb and forefinger of your left hand, pinch the fibers with the tips pointing toward the rear of the hook and anchor them with four to six wraps of the thread around the hook shank. The tail should always be tied just above the bend of the hook so that it sticks out straight behind the fly at the same angle as the hook shank.

CATCH AND RELEASE NOTE
You can reduce the number of inadvertent eye and brain injuries to fish by tying a strip of lead wire along the underside of a fly.

This helps the fly to drift upright in the current, thus reducing the chances of hooking fish through the tender tissues in the roof of the mouth when they take the hook.

Attaching a tail
The tail of the fly is not only important from the point of view of mimicking the appearance of the natural insect, but also as a keel to keep the fly upright and afloat in the water.

4) Finished tail

Applying dubbing

1) Pull off about eight to ten hackle fibers from a strand of saddle hackle.

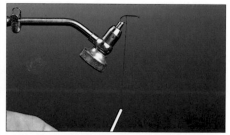

1) Anchor the thread securely and wrap one layer of thread around the shank. Pull the bobbin toward you until there are approximately 5 in. (13 cm.) of thread between the hook and the bobbin.

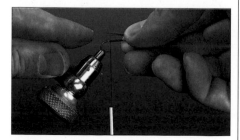

2) Holding them loosely between the thumb and forefinger of your right hand,

2) Using a sticky wax, such as beeswax, stroke the thread four or five times (just enough to make the thread tacky).

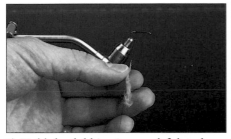

3) Hold the dubbing in your left hand while keeping the thread tight with your right. Gently spin the dubbing onto your thread using a twisting motion made with your thumb and forefinger.

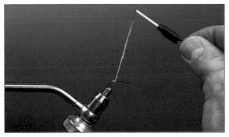

4) Wrap the hook with the spun dubbing to form the body. More wraps will give you a thicker body.

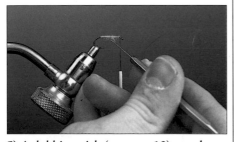

5) A dubbing pick (see page 12) may be used to "tease" the body to achieve life-like appearance of wiggling legs and gills.

Remember: *A little bit of dubbing goes a long way. To achieve a consistent, well tapered body the dubbed section should be slightly thicker than the thread itself.*

Palmering hackle

This is a technique whereby the hackle feather is wrapped around the hook shank so that it spirals forward from the rear of the shank. When hackle feathers are wound around the hook shank, the individual barbules stick out like the bristles of a brush in a spiral formation. Palmered hackle gives the fly a life-like appearance, and emphasizes the effect of shimmering movement. Palmered hackle can be used on dry flies, nymphs, streamers, and emergers. For wet flies and streamers the shiny side of the feather should face toward the front of the hook; for dry flies the shiny side should face the rear of the hook.

1) Anchor the tip of the hackle to the hook and grip the butt of the hackle with your thumb and forefinger or hackle pliers.

2) Wrap the hackle in the same direction as your thread over and around the hook shank. Space the wraps evenly as you work toward the eye of the hook.

3) Anchor the butt of the hackle with five or six wraps of your thread. Clip off the excess hackle.

Wrapping dry fly hackle

Dry-fly hackle typically requires the short, stiff fibers found on a rooster neck. The hackle of a dry fly is wrapped quite closely together, whereas palmered hackle is spiraled more loosely from the rear of the fly to the front with space between each wrap. The tightly bunched hackle of a dry fly helps to support the weight of the fly on the surface of the water and the motion that it imports to the hook as it undulates in the currents of the water imitating the quivering legs of a struggling insect.

1) To anchor a dry-fly hackle, trim the fibers around the butt of the hackle stem and anchor it butt-first to the hook shank. Avoid using the "webby" portion at the bottom of the feather. It is too soft and will all too readily absorb moisture causing the fly to sink.

2) Using your fingertips or hackle pliers, grip the tip of the hackle and wrap it clockwise around the hook shank. Each wrap should touch the previous one.

3) Anchor the tip and clip off excess material.

Creating peacock chenille

To increase its durability, peacock can be spun around your thread to form a type of chenille.

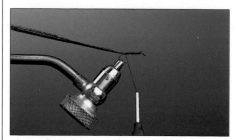

1) Anchor the tips of two or three strands of peacock herl to the hook shank. Maintaining tension, pull off 5 in. (13 cm.) of thread from the bobbin.

2) Gently spin the peacock fibers around the tightened thread with the thumb and forefinger of your left hand in a clockwise motion. Do not wrap the peacock too tightly or it will break.

3) Wrap the desired amount of peacock chenille around the hook shank, anchor it, and clip off any excess.

4) This is how peacock chenille should look when finished.

Parachute wings

These effectively simulate the upright wings of a mayfly and are extremely visible on the water. Virtually any wing material may be used as the "post" to which the parachute wing is attached, but the most commonly used substance is calf tail or calf body hair.

1) Carefully stack a small portion of calf body in your hairstacker. Remove any coarse guard hairs.

2) Anchor the hair (tips forward) to the hook shank. Parachute wings should always be anchored at a point about one third of the length of the shank behind the eye.

3) Once firmly anchored, pull the hair

Finished fly with Parachute wings.

backward and hold it in an upright position to create the post. With your bobbin hand, build up a small ridge directly in front of the post until it remains standing on its own.

4) Circle the post several times with your thread to draw the hairs together and to create a firm base for your hackle wraps. A small drop of head cement dabbed at the base of the post can add to its resiliency and help when it comes to wrapping your hackle.

5) Anchor your hackle butt-first near the base of the post. Wrap the hackle clockwise around the post. Each wrap should go **below** the previous one. This will help to keep the hackle from unraveling over the top of the post.

6) Anchor hackle, clip off any excess, and whip-finish.

Splitting wings

The technique for splitting wings is similar to that used when you make the parachute wings. Once again a variety of materials can be used, but calf body and calf tail are the most common. Follow steps (1–3) for parachute wings. Once the

Finished fly with split wings.

hair is in the upright position, pull it backward and upright to form the post. Build up a ridge in front of the hair to hold it in this position.

4) Carefully divide the hair into two equal sections.

5) Wrap thread around hair in a figure-eight motion so that the two posts stand independently in a "V" shape.

Spinning hair

The task of spinning hair requires stout thread and plenty of patience.

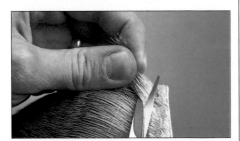

1) Begin by wrapping a thin base of thread around the hook shank.

2) Cut a portion of deer hair (about the diameter of a pencil).

3) Remove any guard hairs or underfur.

4) Lay the hair parallel to the hook shank and make one loose wrap around the bunch with your thread.

5) Make a second wrap directly over the first and slowly cinch up the thread until both wraps are tight. As you tighten the thread, the deer hair will compress and flare out. Allow the hair to turn around the hook so you get a full 360° coverage of the hook shank. If you want to create a full-bodied, buoyant fly, the process may be repeated several more times along the length of the hook shank. Take care to pack the previous bunch of hair, before starting the next cycle.

6) Once the desired amount of hair has been spun onto the hook shank, trim and shape it with scissors.

EXAMPLES OF FINISHED FLIES

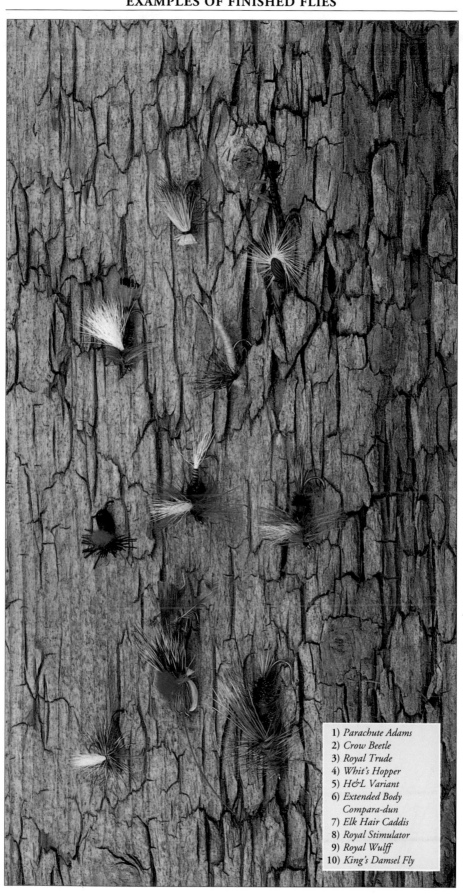

1) *Parachute Adams*
2) *Crow Beetle*
3) *Royal Trude*
4) *Whit's Hopper*
5) *H&L Variant*
6) *Extended Body Compara-dun*
7) *Elk Hair Caddis*
8) *Royal Stimulator*
9) *Royal Wulff*
10) *King's Damsel Fly*

TYING FLIES

THIS CHAPTER focuses on tying actual flies using the techniques and materials demonstrated in the previous pages. Do not be alarmed if your first attempts do not turn out as planned. With a little practice you will soon gain the skills necessary to tie well-proportioned and durable flies. We will progress step-by-step through a variety of flies. Use the illustrations as your guidelines and concentrate on the individual techniques illustrated, rather than the entire fly itself. Once you master the techniques, the flies will take care of themselves.

Girdle Bug

1) Fold one 2 in. (5 cm.) rubber strip in half and anchor it at the rear of the hook shank as the tail.

2) Anchor two more rubber strips so they form an "X" across the top of the hook shank. Adjust them as necessary to make them symmetrical.

Finished Girdle Bug.

3) Repeat this process about one third of the length of the hook shank in front of the first set of legs.

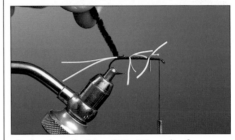

4) Anchor 4–6 in. (10–15 cm.) of chenille to the rear of the hook shank.

5) Wrap the chenille forward positioning each wrap tightly against the one before and snugging them tightly against the rubber legs.

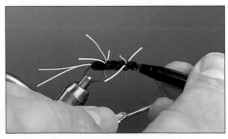

6) Clip excess chenille and whip finish.

The **Bead Head Prince Nymph** combines the best attributes of a beauty queen and an old Chevy truck. It not only looks good, but you can count on it to get the job done. It is a very productive fly for both trout and panfish.

1) Slip the bead over the bend of the hook (you may have to pinch the barb to help it fit).

2) Measure two brown goose biots against the length of the hook gap, and anchor them so they "fork" apart.

3) Attach 2 in. (5 cm.) of gold wire or tinsel at the rear of the hook.

4) Anchor three pieces of peacock herl with five or six wraps of thread, and create a piece of peacock chenille (see pages 30–31 in the techniques section).

5) Wrap the peacock chenille up to the bead. Anchor it, and clip off any excess peacock that may be attached.

6) Counter-rib the peacock by wrapping your wire or tinsel counterclockwise around the peacock to give it additional strength and durability.

7) Attach two white goose biots to the top of the fly in such a manner that they form a "V" shape.

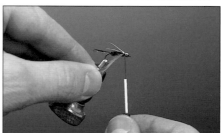

8) Make one wrap of brown hackle just behind the bead and sweep the fibers toward the rear of the hook using the thumb and forefinger of your left hand.

The finished fly. Remember to clip away excess hackle and whip-finish.

Bead Head flies are excellent at grabbing the trout's attention.

The **Royal Wulff** is a favorite among fishermen in the western U.S. for its visibility and buoyancy—especially in rough water. Although created by the great fly fisherman Lee Wulff as a trout fly, the Royal Wulff isn't shy about fooling panfish as well.

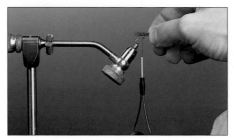

1) Anchor a small amount of stacked moose or elk hair as the tail.

2) Stack and split a portion of calf body or calf tail hair for the wings as shown on page 31 in the techniques section.

3) Create peacock chenille with three strands of peacock herl and wrap twice around the hook shank.

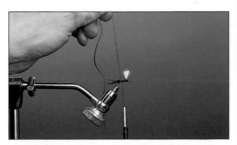

4) Anchor a short piece of red floss and overwrap the peacock using six or seven repetitions.

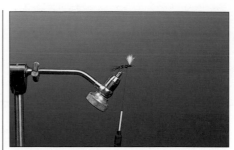

5) Continue wrapping the peacock chenille for two more wraps—or until you reach the edge of the wings, and anchor it.

6) Attach the butts of two hackles directly behind the wings—remembering to keep the shiny side forward.

7) Using hackle pliers or simply your fingers, grip the tips of the hackles and wrap them toward the eye of the hook—snugging the hackles up closely to the wings of the fly.

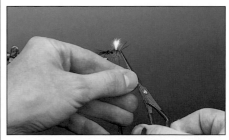

8) Anchor the hackles, clip off excess, and whip-finish.

A finished Royal Wulff.

The Royal Wulff is a favorite among anglers for its visibility and buoyancy.

The **Bass Popper** can be tied in virtually any color to imitate frogs, mice, or wounded fish. Many anglers will argue whether a bass is really eating a popper out of hunger or attacking it out of aggression. Regardless, few things are more exciting than watching the explosive strikes of largemouth bass as they inhale a deer-hair popper.

4) Spin the deer hair from the hackle to a point one third along the length of the hook shank and tie in four rubber legs tight to the spun deer hair.

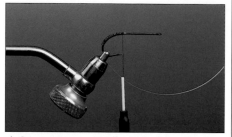

1) Secure Mason 20 lb. (9 kg.) hard nylon monofilament to the rear of the hook to serve as the weed guard. The stiff monofilament forms a loop from the front of the fly to the rear. The loop hangs down below the fly, and is rigid enough to prevent the hook from snagging on weeds, but will still allow it to penetrate the mouth of a striking fish.

5) Spin the hair along the next third of the hook shank and add four more rubber legs to match the four that you have already attached. Finish spinning the deer hair to the eye of the hook and trim away excess hair with a razor. Secure the weed guard to the eye of the hook. Finish spinning hair to the eye of the hook and trim away excess hair with scissors or a razor.

2) Attach four saddle-hackle feathers butt-first to the rear of the hook as the tail. The tail should protrude approximately 2 in. (5 cm.) behind the bend of the hook.

Note: Experiment with different colors when tying your deer-hair poppers and even try alternating colors as you spin the hair. Suggested colors: green/black, yellow/black, white/black, chartreuse/black, or all black.

A finished Bass Popper fly.

(3) Anchor three more saddle-hackle feathers and palmer them dry-fly-style.

The **Woolly Bugger** is the meat and potatoes of fly-fishing. It can be tied in a variety of sizes and colors, and it has proved itself attractive to multitudes of fish. There's nothing fancy about it, but it sure is appealing. The Woolly Bugger is probably the most commonly used fly in America today—simply because it works. Woolly Buggers may be tied in any color you like, although black, brown, and olive are the most common. The Woolly Bugger can be used for virtually any fish that swims including trout, bass, and pike.

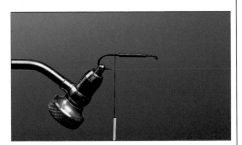

1) Weight the hook with a brass bead, lead barbell eyes, or lead wire.

2) Attach two marabou feathers to the rear of the hook shank. You may want to add some crystal flash with the marabou for added sparkle.

Note: For increased strength and flash you can add a strip of wire at this point that may be used to counter-rib the chenille and hackle once they are in place.

A finished Woolly Bugger.

3) Attach a piece of chenille approximately 4 in. (10 cm.) long and make one wrap.

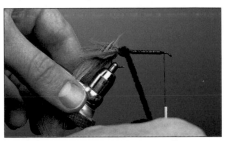

4) Anchor one saddle hackle, tip first as illustrated.

5) Wrap the thread and chenille to the front of the hook. Anchor the chenille.

6) Palmer the hackle forward.

7) Anchor hackle, clip off excess, and whip-finish.

Another trout brought to hand through the good work of the Woolly Bugger.

The **Pike Bunny** exhibits the same shimmering movement underwater as a live fish and offers little chance of escape to the toothy predator that pursues it. Pike are perhaps the most aggressive of all freshwater game fish and will pursue virtually any fly that is tied to imitate baitfish. They are very opportunistic feeders, seizing on all sorts of available prey to satisfy their voracious appetites.

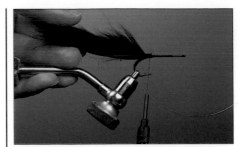

2) Anchor four saddle-hackle feathers with several strands of crystal flash to the rear of the hook as the tail.

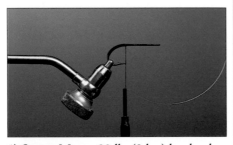

1) Secure Mason 20 lb. (9 kg.) hard nylon monofilament to the rear of the hook for the weed guard.

3) Anchor a thin strip of rabbit to the rear of the hook.

(4) Palmer the strip forward as if it were a hackle fiber and anchor it just behind the eye of the hook.

(5) Secure weed guard to the front of the hook and clip excess.

A finished Pike Bunny.

Below *When an aggressive pike strikes, hold on to your hat. These are big fish, and they can put up a tremendous fight when hooked. They are often found near weedbeds where they lurk in wait for their prey.*

Glossary

Abdomen Generally referred to as the posterior portion of the insect's body, behind the thorax.

Body The portion of the fly that covers the entire hook shank. The body may be separated into the abdomen and the thorax.

Dry flies Imitate the adult (winged) stage of aquatic insects or terrestrials. Dry flies are fished on the surface of the water and are tied with hackle, foam, buoyant hair follicles, or other

Parachute Adams.

synthetic materials to help support the weight of the fly. Most dry fly-fishing (excluding that using bass/pike poppers) utilizes a "dead drift" technique so that the angler imparts no foreign movement or action to the fly which is allowed to drift freely with the current.

Dubbing A technique of spinning fur or a synthetic substitute onto the thread and then wrapping it around the hook shank to form the body, thorax, or head. The term dubbing may also be used to denote the actual fur or synthetic alternative employed.

Emerger The transitional phase of an aquatic insect as it changes from the nymph to the adult form. As the nymph swims, floats, or crawls to the surface it is termed an "emerger."

Fiber An individual follicle of a feather.

Grizzly hackle Hackle color named for the white and black barring pattern on the feathers.

Guard hairs The longer, stiffer fibers found in most natural fur dubbing, such as rabbit, squirrel, and muskrat. Natural fur dubbing with an abundance of guard hairs is excellent for

Muskrat fur.

tying nymphs where numerous legs and gills are simulated.

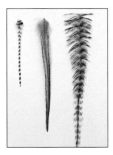

Hackle A single feather from either a neck or saddle cape of a bird. The term "hackle" may also be used to denote the portion of the fly that is wrapped with the hackle itself.

Nymph The immature (unwinged) stage of an aquatic insect. The life of a nymph is spent underwater for periods of one to three years (dependent upon

Red Bellied Girdle Fly.

the species). Nymph imitations are commonly fished with a weight to help them to sink rapidly. Most nymph fishing utilizes a "dead drift" so that the angler imparts no foreign movement or action and the fly is allowed to drift freely with the current.

Palmered Hackle The technique of wrapping a hackle around the fly in a spiral motion causing the hackle to stick out like bristles on a bottle-brush. Palmered hackle can give undulating lifelike movement to a nymph or streamer and can add buoyancy and the appearance of legs to a dry fly.

Quill/stem The central shaft of a feather from which the individual fibers sprout.

Rib The technique of wrapping floss, wire, or tinsel around the body of a fly to give it additional strength, flash, or the appearance of segmentation.

Shell-back The hard outer layer found on freshwater shrimp, scuds, and crayfish.

Spinning or spun hair The technique of wrapping stiff hair, such as deer or elk, with stout thread and pulling it tight so that the individual hair follicles flare out and away from the body. This technique is used for making the heads and bodies of many bass flies, grasshopper patterns, and Muddler Minnows.

Streamer A baitfish, frog, or crayfish imitation that is fished actively with some type of retrieval motion that causes the fly to move in a life-like manner.

Streamer Woolly Bugger.

Stripping line A technique used in streamer fishing in which the fly is actively retrieved to simulate the movements of a fleeing or panicked baitfish.

Terrestrials Land-born insects, such as grasshoppers, beetles, ants, and caterpillars.

Thorax The thickest portion of the insect, just behind the head, from which the legs protrude and the wings develop.

Weed guard Mainly fitted to bass, pike, and panfish flies, weed guards are used to keep the hook point free of weeds, moss, or other obstructions. Weed guards may be constructed from piano wire or stiff nylon monofilament.

Wet fly A fly that imitates an emerging insect or which may be used as an attractor pattern that preys on the natural curiosity of the fish. Wet flies typically have swept-back wings and sparse hackle. As the name suggests, wet flies are fished below the surface of the water.

Whip finish The final knot applied to the fly to keep the thread from unraveling. A half hitch may also be used as a substitute for the whip finish.

Wing case This nymphal structure, located on top of the thorax, houses the unfurled, developing wings of an aquatic insect.

CONCLUSION

I F YOU have read this Workstation on tying flies carefully and methodically, you should by now have aquired a basic understanding of the craft of tying flies. Of course, it is a skill that you never stop learning, but once the fundamentals have been grasped, you will have a very sound base on which you can build.

Remember that fly-tying at its simplest level is merely a blend of basic techniques. Once these techniques have been mastered, they can be combined with different materials to create a huge variety of flies. Hopefully your appetite has been whetted and your fingers are itching to start tying flies. Good luck and good fishing.

REFERENCE FILE

THE FINAL CHAPTER of this book is a "recipe" section that gives you ingredients for some of the more popular flies in production today. For your convenience the flies are marked individually for their uses: **T=Trout, P=Panfish, B=Bass,** and **PK=Pike**. As you will notice many of the flies are extremely versatile and may be used for a variety of applications. The tear-out format allows you to take any page to your local fly shop or craft store as a type of grocery list. By using the techniques demonstrated in the previous chapters you will have the information and skills necessary to tie all of the following flies. As a final note, if you do not have a convenient source of fly-tying materials or tools, the following shops will gladly ship you any of the tools and materials you may need to continue your fly-tying.

The Rivers Edge
2012 N. 7th Ave.
Bozeman, MT 59715
(406) 586-5373

Bob Marriott's Flyfishing Store
2700 W. Orangethorpe
Fullerton, CA 92633
(714) 525-1827

The Flyfisher
252 Clayton St.
Denver, CO 80206
(303) 322-5014

Florida Keys Outfitters
81920 Overseas Hwy.
Islamorada, FL 33036
(305) 664-5423

The Fish Hawk
283 Buckhead Ave.
Atalanta, GA 30305
(404) 233-5065

Gates Ausable Lodge Stephan Bridge
Rt. 2, Box 2
Grayling, MI 49738
(517) 348-8462

Ramsey Outdoor Stores
226 Route 17
Paramus, NJ 07652
(201) 261-5000

Kaufmann's Streamborn
P.O. Box 23032
Portland, OR 97223
(503) 639-6400

The Austin Angler
312 1/2 Congress Ave.
Austin, TX 78701
(512) 472-4553

Urban Angler Ltd.
118 E. 25th St.
New York, NY 10010
(212) 979-7600

NYMPHS

HARE'S EAR NYMPH *T/P*

Hook	10-20 Dai Riki 730
Tail	Hare's mask guard hair
Rib	Gold tinsel or wire
Body	Hare's mask
Thorax	Hare's mask
Wing case	Turkey flat

NYMPHS

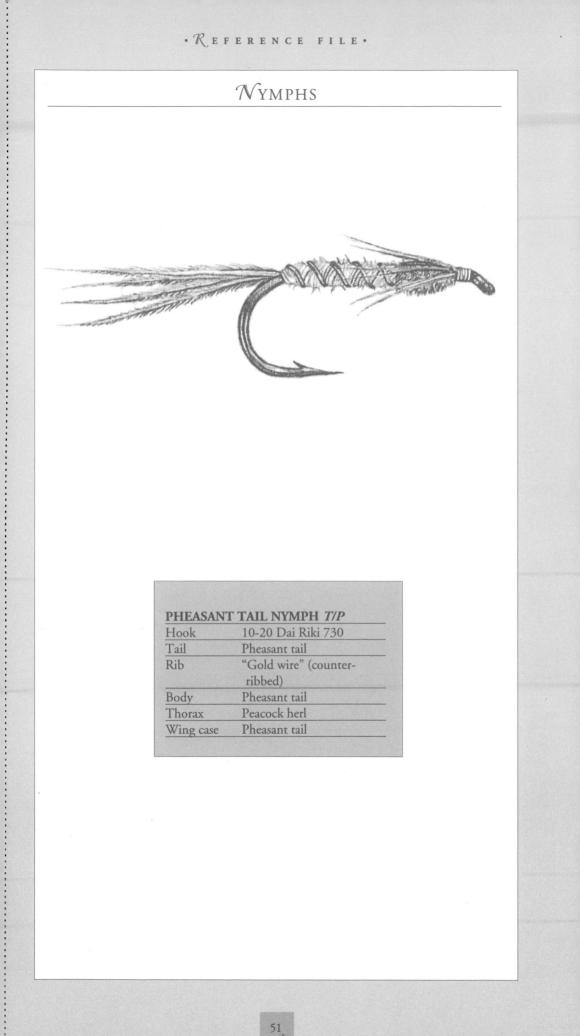

PHEASANT TAIL NYMPH *TIP*

Hook	10-20 Dai Riki 730
Tail	Pheasant tail
Rib	"Gold wire" (counter-ribbed)
Body	Pheasant tail
Thorax	Peacock herl
Wing case	Pheasant tail

NYMPHS

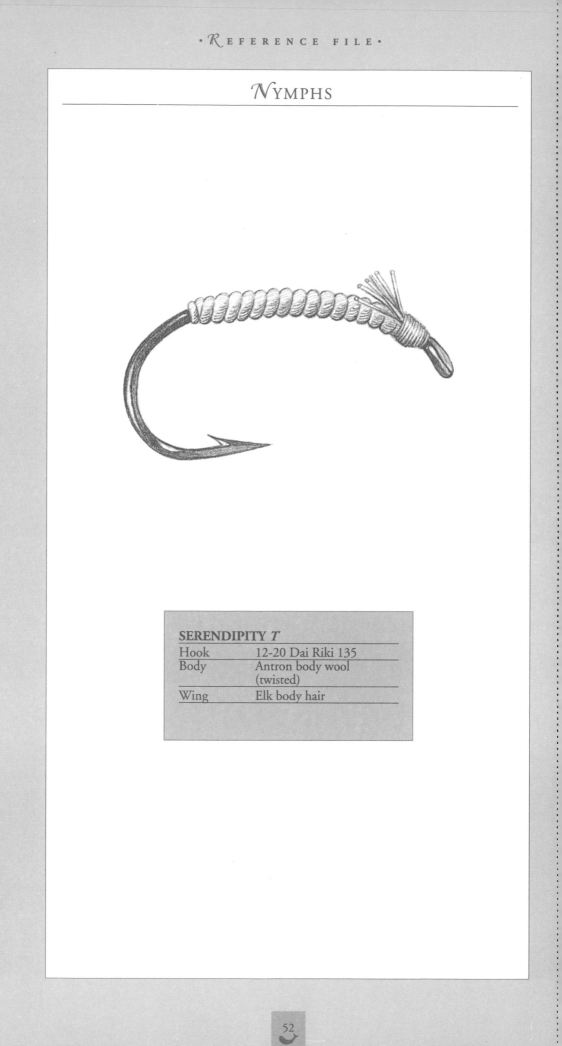

SERENDIPITY T

Hook	12-20 Dai Riki 135
Body	Antron body wool (twisted)
Wing	Elk body hair

NYMPHS

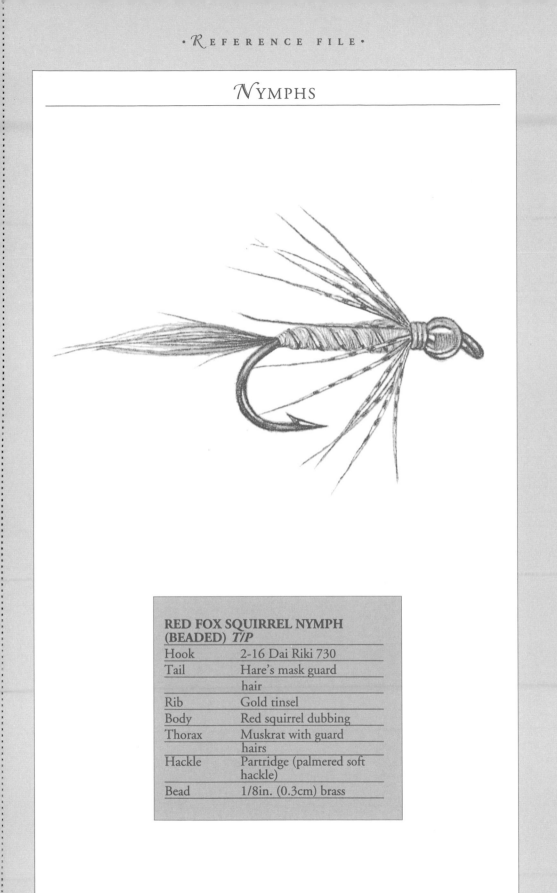

RED FOX SQUIRREL NYMPH (BEADED) *T/P*

Hook	2-16 Dai Riki 730
Tail	Hare's mask guard hair
Rib	Gold tinsel
Body	Red squirrel dubbing
Thorax	Muskrat with guard hairs
Hackle	Partridge (palmered soft hackle)
Bead	1/8in. (0.3cm) brass

NYMPHS

PEACOCK SOFT HACKLE (BEADED) *T/P*

Hook	12-16 Dai Riki 135
Body	Peacock herl
Hackle	Partridge (palmered soft hackle)
Thread	Red 6/0
Bead	1/8 in. (0.3 cm.) brass

DRY FLIES

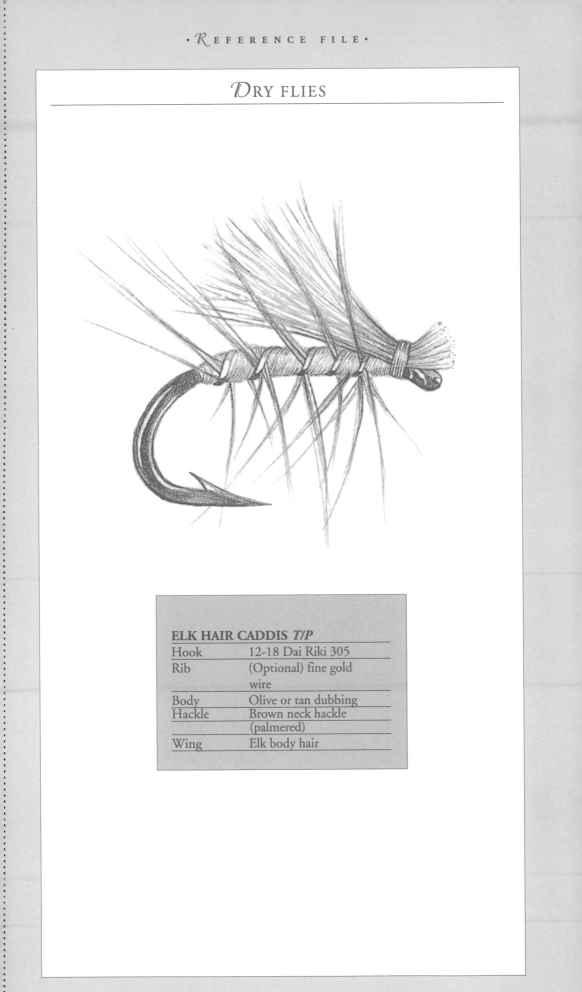

ELK HAIR CADDIS *T/P*

Hook	12-18 Dai Riki 305
Rib	(Optional) fine gold wire
Body	Olive or tan dubbing
Hackle	Brown neck hackle (palmered)
Wing	Elk body hair

DRY FLIES

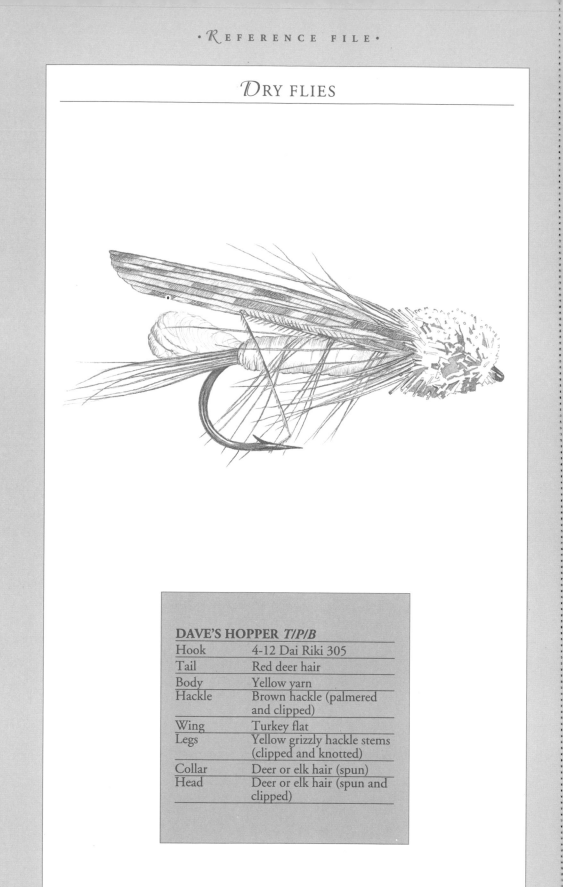

DAVE'S HOPPER *T/P/B*

Hook	4-12 Dai Riki 305
Tail	Red deer hair
Body	Yellow yarn
Hackle	Brown hackle (palmered and clipped)
Wing	Turkey flat
Legs	Yellow grizzly hackle stems (clipped and knotted)
Collar	Deer or elk hair (spun)
Head	Deer or elk hair (spun and clipped)

DRY FLIES

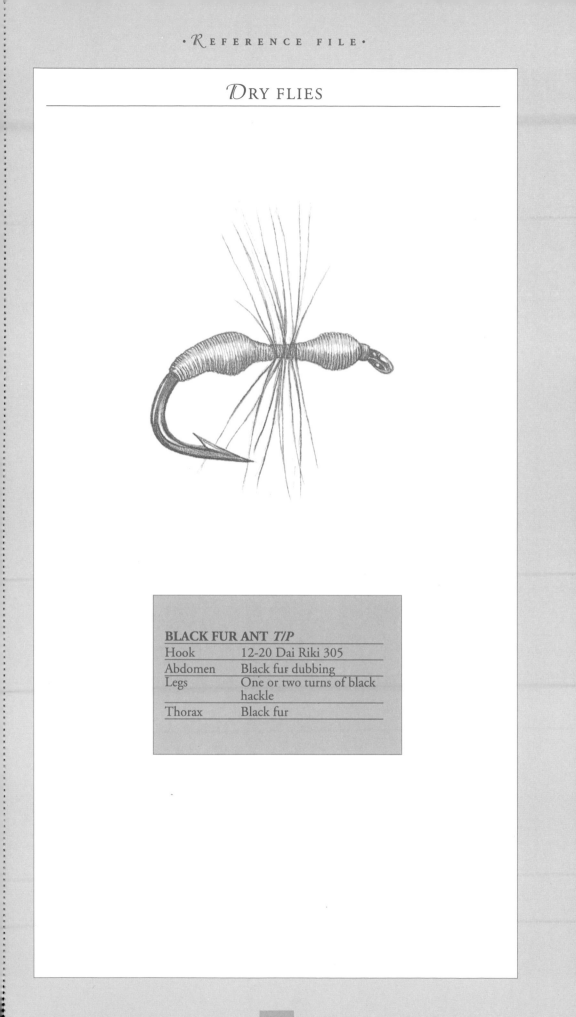

BLACK FUR ANT *T/P*

Hook	12-20 Dai Riki 305
Abdomen	Black fur dubbing
Legs	One or two turns of black hackle
Thorax	Black fur

DRY FLIES

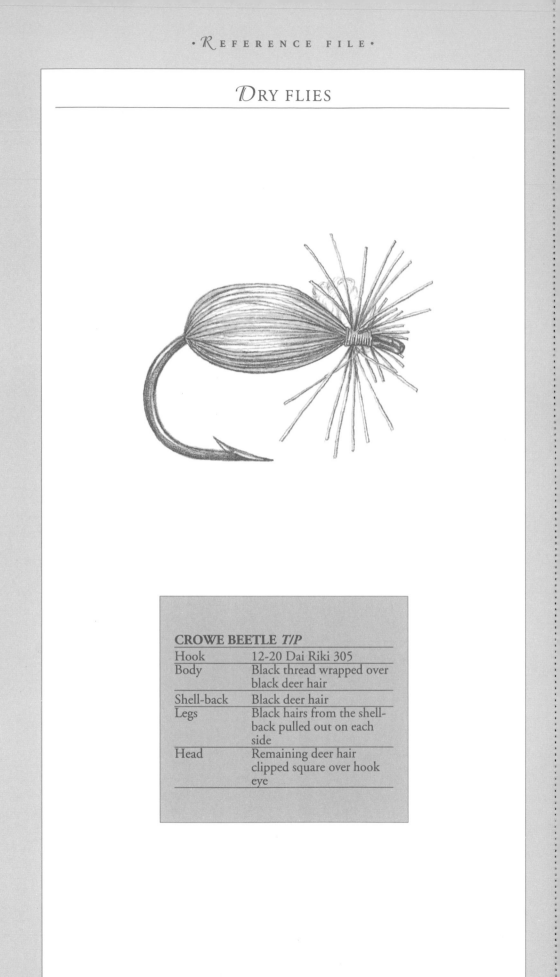

CROWE BEETLE *T/P*

Hook	12-20 Dai Riki 305
Body	Black thread wrapped over black deer hair
Shell-back	Black deer hair
Legs	Black hairs from the shell-back pulled out on each side
Head	Remaining deer hair clipped square over hook eye

STREAMERS

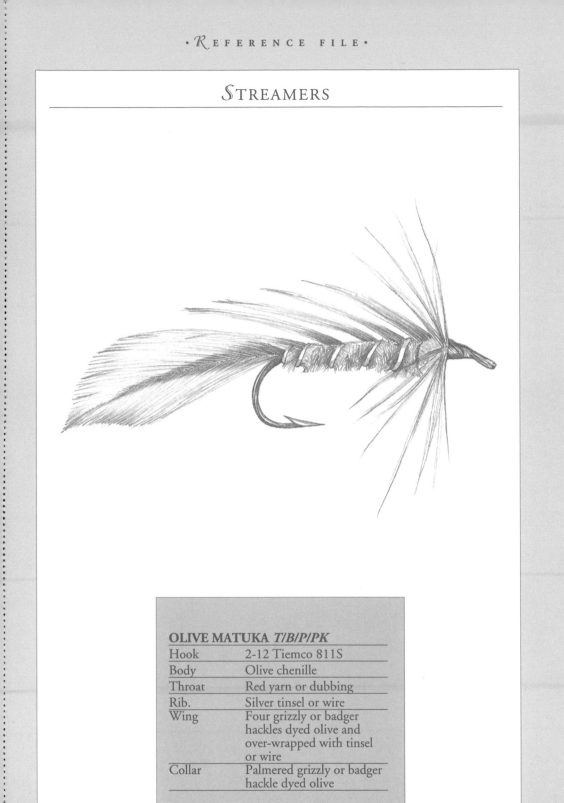

OLIVE MATUKA *T/B/P/PK*

Hook	2-12 Tiemco 811S
Body	Olive chenille
Throat	Red yarn or dubbing
Rib.	Silver tinsel or wire
Wing	Four grizzly or badger hackles dyed olive and over-wrapped with tinsel or wire
Collar	Palmered grizzly or badger hackle dyed olive

STREAMERS

MUDDLER MINNOW *T/P/B/PK*

Hook	2-10 Dai Riki 730
Tail	Turkey quill
Body	Gold tinsel
Underwing	Gray squirrel tail
Wing	Turkey quill
Collar	Deer hair (spun)
Head	Deer hair (spun and clipped)

STREAMERS

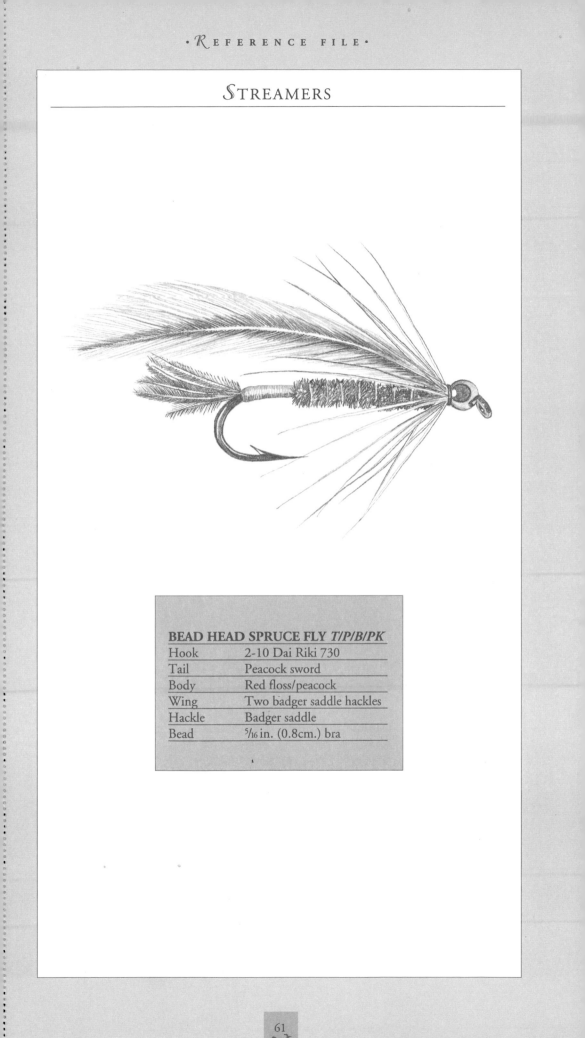

BEAD HEAD SPRUCE FLY *T/P/B/PK*

Hook	2-10 Dai Riki 730
Tail	Peacock sword
Body	Red floss/peacock
Wing	Two badger saddle hackles
Hackle	Badger saddle
Bead	5/16 in. (0.8cm.) bra

STREAMERS

RIVERS EDGE CRAYFISH T/B/P

Hook	2-6 Streamer, 6x long
Tail	Squirrel fanned from shell-back and clipped
Body	Medium olive chenille
Shellback	Squirrel tail brought back from pincers
Hackle	Brown or furnace saddle hackle
Eyes	Black barbell eyes
Pincers	Squirrel, separated and shaped

STREAMERS

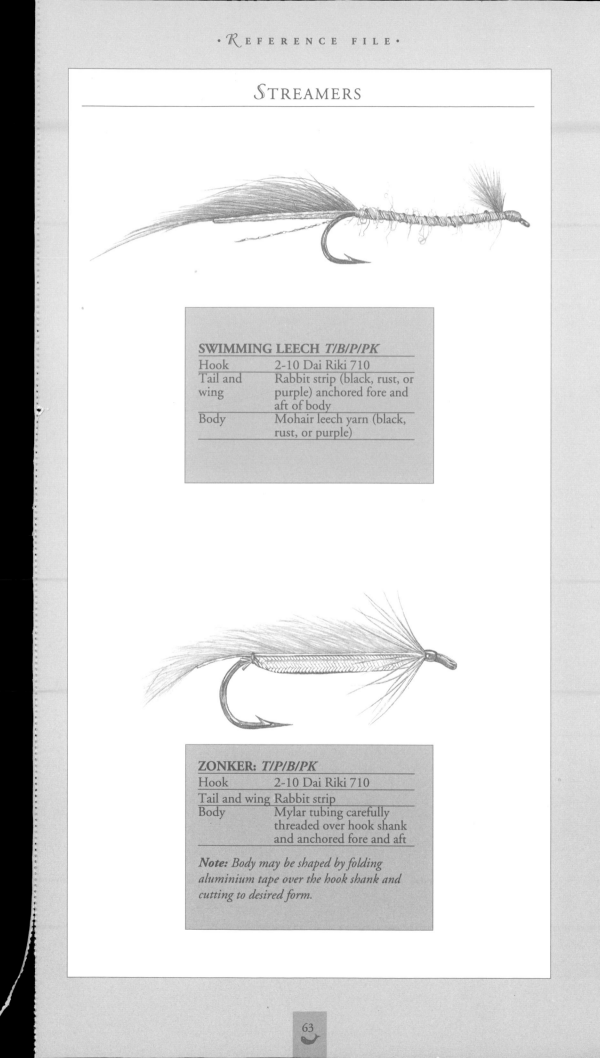

SWIMMING LEECH *T/B/P/PK*

Hook	2-10 Dai Riki 710
Tail and wing	Rabbit strip (black, rust, or purple) anchored fore and aft of body
Body	Mohair leech yarn (black, rust, or purple)

ZONKER: *T/P/B/PK*

Hook	2-10 Dai Riki 710
Tail and wing	Rabbit strip
Body	Mylar tubing carefully threaded over hook shank and anchored fore and aft

Note: Body may be shaped by folding aluminium tape over the hook shank and cutting to desired form.

STREAMERS

KICKER FROG *P/B/PK*	
Hook	2-6 Tiemco 300
Legs	Green over yellow bucktail (wire is placed in the middle of the leg, over-wrapped with tying thread and then bent to shape)
Body	Green spun deer hair on top, yellow on bottom
Eyes	Doll's eyes